JOHN GRANT

Littlenose Goes South

HODDER AND STOUGHTON
London Sydney Auckland Toronto

British Library Cataloguing in Publication Data

Grant, John, *1930–*
Littlenose goes south.
I. Title II. Series
823′.914 [J]

ISBN 0-340-51412-4

First published 1990

Published by Hodder and Stoughton Children's Books, a division of Hodder and Stoughton Ltd, Mill Road, Dunton Green, Sevenoaks, Kent TN13 2YA

Photoset by Litho Link Ltd, Welshpool, Powys, Wales

Printed in Great Britain by St Edmundsbury Press Ltd, Bury St Edmunds, Suffolk

Contents

Over the Hills and Far Away

Chapter 1

At the end of the last Ice Age – that is, about fifty thousand years ago – the Neanderthal Folk lived in caves, wore furs and hunted animals for food. They were *very* handsome people, proud of their large, red, snuffly noses. Except Littlenose! His nose was no bigger than a berry. He lived in the family cave with Father, Mother and Two-Eyes, his pet mammoth, and was never happier than when he was up to mischief of some sort or other, or playing tricks on the other members of the tribe.

One morning Littlenose stepped from the cave, and shivered. There were patches of frost on the grass, and his breath came in white puffs. So he went back inside and reappeared wearing his winter furs. There was a loud honking from the sky as a large flock of geese flew high overhead.

'Sensible birds,' said Littlenose to himself. 'Who wants to stay around here during another ice-age winter? Not me, for one!'

He cheered up when he remembered

that Uncle Redhead was coming for a few days. Uncle Redhead arrived just before lunch. As he sat down to eat with Father, Mother and Littlenose, he said, 'I picked up an interesting little gadget on my last trip south. I must show it to you. It could be quite revolutionary in its way.'

Littlenose pricked up his ears. Father only grunted.

While Mother cleared away the lunch things, Uncle Redhead led the others outside and across the open ground in front of the cave. Then, from his travelling pack, he produced a piece of wood.

'Oh, yes!' said Father. 'Very revolutionary. Things will never be the same after this!'

Uncle Redhead ignored him, and let Littlenose have a closer look. The piece of wood was thin and flat and as wide as three fingers. It was also bent, a bit like a crescent moon, but not so smoothly curved.

'What does it do?' asked Littlenose.

'It comes back,' said Uncle Redhead. 'If I throw it, it will come back to me, and I won't have the bother of running after it to get it back.'

Father said, 'You could save yourself a lot of bother if you didn't throw it in the first place!'

Uncle Redhead put on a patient expression. 'It's for hunting,' he said. 'Suppose you throw it at a rabbit and miss . . . '

Father interrupted. 'I never miss,' he said.

That, thought Littlenose, is true. Father is a first-class hunter. Just like he's always telling me.

'I'll show you,' said Uncle Redhead.

He gripped the piece of wood by one end, drew back his arm, and threw hard. The piece of wood spun through the air, and just when Littlenose thought it ought to fall to the ground it soared upwards, twisting and turning before swooping back towards where they stood. Uncle Redhead reached out to catch it. But, he didn't reach far enough. There was a shriek from inside the cave as it whizzed past Mother's nose.

'Where did it go? Where did it go?' cried Uncle Redhead, dashing inside.

Mother pointed to the fire where Uncle Redhead's revolutionary gadget was crackling merrily among the flames.

'I think it's easier carrying in an armful of

firewood like we've always done,' she said.

Uncle Redhead was rather downcast, but not for long. 'Mustn't waste time playing about,' he said. 'Got a lot to do before I head south for the winter.'

'Like the geese?' said Littlenose.

'Except that we can't fly, yes,' said Uncle Redhead.

'What's it like? South, I mean?' asked Littlenose.

'More wonderful than you can imagine,' said Uncle Redhead. 'The sun is so hot that it can burn you if you are not careful. And there are trees and fruits and flowers the likes of which you've never seen. There are fruits sweeter than the sweetest honey, and round and golden as the sun itself.'

The afternoon air was mild, and Mother, Father and Two-Eyes joined Littlenose while Uncle Redhead talked of the wonders of the southlands.

'Are there mammoths and rhinoceros?' asked Littlenose.

'Yes,' said his uncle.

Father laughed. 'If it's really as hot as

you say, they would melt in their fur!'

'They don't wear fur,' said Uncle Redhead.

'Really!' exclaimed Mother. 'Do you mean to tell me that they go about absolutely . . . ? Oh, dear! Not in front of Littlenose! And Two-Eyes is blushing. The tip of his trunk has gone quite pink!'

So Uncle Redhead told them about the people instead. They had brown skins, and some were even black, but Uncle Redhead had only heard of them. He hadn't seen them for himself.

As he described all those strange things, other members of the tribe gathered round to listen. The air had turned cold with the coming evening when Uncle Redhead stopped. The Neanderthal Folk gave Uncle Redhead a round of applause before going home to their caves. Father didn't join in the clapping.

'What a load of old rubbish!' he exclaimed. 'Naked mammoths, golden fruit, black people!'

But Littlenose didn't think it all a load of old rubbish. He lay awake that night thinking about all that his uncle had said, and fell asleep to dream of the strange and wonderful southlands.

In the morning, Littlenose made up his mind. After breakfast he asked Uncle Redhead, 'Could I come with you when you go south?'

Uncle Redhead said, 'Why not?'

Father grunted!

And Mother said, 'Oh, dear!'

'I think it's a great idea,' said Uncle Redhead. 'I could do with a bit of company when I'm travelling. Bring Two-Eyes. He can help carry our gear.'

Two-Eyes wasn't so pleased at that. He fancied going south to see the strange mammoths with no fur, but . . . well, he couldn't have everything. The Old Man, leader of the tribe, came along at that

moment to discuss some hunting arrangements with Father. But when he heard that Littlenose might be going south with Uncle Redhead he cried, 'Wonderful! What an opportunity! I went south myself when I was Littlenose's age. Ah, happy days!'

And that settled it. Even Father didn't dare object when the Old Man approved. In fact, it was made official! The Old Man called a meeting. 'Ladies and gentlemen,' he said, 'our most junior hunter will shortly venture on a journey undertaken by very few. He will carry the fame of our tribe into lands as yet unknown.'

He went on like that for a long time, while the Neanderthal Folk nodded agreement. This is all getting a bit out of hand, thought Littlenose. I thought I was going on holiday with Uncle Redhead!

Preparations for the journey started that very day. Everyone had a lot of advice to give, but Uncle Redhead said, 'We will travel light. Hunting robes, spears, flint knives, fire-making flints, and hunting bags to carry everything.'

At length all the gear was checked, packed and ready. The Old Man had ordered a farewell feast, with Littlenose and Uncle Redhead as guests of honour. Littlenose felt strange, sitting with Uncle Redhead beside the Old Man while the whole tribe ate and drank and were entertained with songs and dancing. The Old Man made one of his speeches, although Littlenose heard very little of it as he had fallen asleep. Then it was time for a good night's sleep before an early start next day.

When I go to sleep tomorrow night I shall be on my way south, Littlenose thought, as he pulled the fur covers over himself.

Mother was a bit sniffly at breakfast,

but Littlenose was too excited to notice. The whole tribe gathered to see them off. And, again, the Old Man made a speech. 'It will be very quiet without Littlenose,' he said.

'Good!' said a voice from the crowd.

The hunting bags and hunting robes were slung on Two-Eyes' back, and amid loud cheering and cries of 'Goodbye' and 'Good luck!' Littlenose, Two-Eyes and Uncle Redhead set their faces to the south and started on their way.

To begin with the journey was through familiar country. They crossed the river and climbed the long slope to the high moors. They skirted the dark pine forest and picked their way carefully across the wide marshlands.

At noon they stopped to eat. The sun was high in the sky. Uncle Redhead pointed to it. 'South lies that way. As long as we are facing the sun at noon, we are going in the right direction.'

Littlenose stood for a moment looking south. All of a sudden something caught his eye ... something moving in a patch of shoulder-high grass. Something big! He beckoned silently to Uncle Redhead. 'What do you think it is?' he whispered.

Uncle Redhead didn't have time to reply. They saw immediately what it was as the grass parted and a huge woolly rhinoceros trotted out, sniffing the air. It was some distance away and didn't see them for a moment. Then it took a few steps forward. And a few more. It began to trot. Then run. As it broke into a gallop, Uncle Redhead shouted, 'Stand still . . . and don't panic!'

He grabbed his hunting robe and hooked the hood over the end of his spear. Then, with a yell he ran towards the charging rhino, waving the robe like a banner. In astonishment, the rhino skidded to a halt and sat down with an earth-shaking thump. And, as Uncle Redhead came on, yelling and waving, it scrambled to its feet and raced off into the long grass until it was lost to view.

'The woolly rhinoceros is just a big bully and a coward,' said Uncle Redhead, unhooking the robe from the end of his spear. 'I learned that trick from a chap I used to know.'

'Used to?' said Littlenose.

'Yes,' said Uncle Redhead. 'That trick

only works on woolly rhinoceroses.
He tried it on a sabre-toothed tiger!'

They loaded up their gear on to Two-Eyes, and set off once again. They left the flatlands and began to climb the foothills. They had reached the beginning of the mountains when Uncle Redhead decided to make camp for the night. Littlenose looked back the way they had come. He thought that far away he could see the smoke from his tribe's cooking fires.
He wondered for a moment if it had been such a good idea after all . . . going south with Uncle Redhead. But it was too late now to change his mind.

Tomorrow his big adventure would really begin.

Down the River
Chapter 2

It was still dark when Uncle Redhead shook Littlenose awake. Two-Eyes munched grass while Uncle Redhead loaded him with the hunting bags.

'Breakfast while we march,' said Uncle Redhead. He handed Littlenose some cold meat and a couple of apples. 'It saves time.' He pointed towards the distant mountains. A valley showed as a tiny notch between two peaks. 'That's where we're bound,' he said. And before he was really properly awake, Littlenose found himself trudging through the cold dawn behind his uncle and Two-Eyes.

At noon the sun shone directly in their faces, so they were still going south.

Littlenose shivered. 'I thought it got warmer as you got farther south,' he said.

'It will,' said Uncle Redhead, 'but it will get a lot colder before that.'

And he was right. They sheltered for the night among some rocks, out of the icy wind. But in spite of his fur hunting robe and a fire burning at his feet, Littlenose lay and shivered until it was time to rise and begin another day's march.

It was more than a week before they stood in the valley between the two mountain peaks.

'It's downhill all the way from here,' said Uncle Redhead. 'The worst part is over.'

Littlenose looked back down the way they had come, and shivered at the memory. They had slipped and slithered over icy rocks, and bowed their heads against driving snow. They had raced for their lives as an avalanche swept over the trail. They had trudged across what seemed an endless snowfield, while giant eagles circled overhead. And they had crouched, holding their breath, among the ice at the foot of a glacier when Uncle Redhead had whispered 'Bigfoot!'
The grey, hairy creatures sniffed and snuffled suspiciously before going on their way. After that it was a breathless climb to the valley.

Pools of icy water lay on the valley floor. A small stream flowed from one to another. After the last pool it was a sizeable river.

‘We follow the river,’ said Uncle Redhead.

For a time the river flowed fast on their left-hand. Then it went over in a roaring waterfall to flow along the foot of a deep ravine.

‘We have to cross the river soon,’ said Uncle Redhead. ‘I hope that it’s still there.’

‘The river?’ asked Littlenose.

‘No,’ said his uncle. ‘The log bridge. It was looking decidedly shaky the last time I came this way. We’ll find out tomorrow. We’ll make camp here tonight. Take your spear and get something for supper.’

While Uncle Redhead unloaded Two-Eyes and got busy with the fire-lighting flints and a pile of twigs, Littlenose crept off among the trees. By the time that Uncle Redhead has a good fire blazing, Littlenose was back with a brace of plump rabbits.

After their supper of roast rabbit (Two-Eyes had some apples), they lay by the fire and Littlenose asked Uncle Redhead to tell him more about the wonderful lands to the south.

Uncle Redhead told him again about the sweet fruits and the perfumed breezes and the warm blue sea. 'It's not all good, however,' he said. 'Some of the tribes can be a bit unpleasant. And there are still a lot of dangerous animals. And . . . there's Old Grumbler!'

'Who's he?' asked Littlenose.

'No one knows,' said Uncle Redhead. 'But he's very short-tempered. And very strong. He must be strong as he can shake the very ground under you for a long way round the mountain where he lives.'

'He lives on a mountain?' asked Littlenose.

'He lives *in* a mountain,' said Uncle

Redhead. 'The light from his fire can be seen from a long way off at night, and the smoke during the day. And, when he's *really* mad he hurls red-hot rocks about. The tribes in that part are afraid of him.'

'I'm not surprised,' said Littlenose. 'Are we going that way?'

'Yes,' said Uncle Redhead. 'Our route takes us quite close to his mountain. I just hope that no one does anything to annoy him.'

Littlenose fell asleep that night with his mind made up that he for one would tip-toe quietly past Old Grumbler's mountain.

The log bridge was not far from where they had made camp. Uncle Redhead unslung his hunting bag from Two-Eyes.

He stepped on to the tree-trunk and started to cross. The top of the log was broad and worn smooth, but it swayed and lurched and pieces of bark and dead twigs dropped off into the ravine. He reached the other side and shouted back to Littlenose, 'Take your bag off Two-Eyes. That will make him lighter. He will cross next.'

Two-Eyes didn't look down. He didn't look anywhere. He walked across the trembling tree bridge with his eyes tight shut. He only opened them when he felt grass under his feet.

Littlenose hitched his hunting bag across his shoulder, took a deep breath, and stepped out. The log, which had swayed when Uncle Redhead crossed, seemed to be coming loose. Littlenose stopped to regain his balance, but he had only taken a couple more steps when the log rolled under him and he toppled off. He made a wild grab at a stump of broken branch. Then he was hanging by one hand over the river far below, the other hand clutching the sling of his hunting bag.

'Don't move!' shouted Uncle Redhead. He pulled a coil of rawhide rope from his bag. He quickly tied a loop in one end and threw it towards Littlenose so that it

dangled beside him. 'Put your foot in the loop!' shouted Uncle Redhead.

Littlenose let the rope take his weight. He started to pull himself by one hand back on to the log. And the stump of broken branch broke! As he fell the loop tightened round his ankle and he stopped with a jerk, dangling upside-down, the hunting bag still clutched in one hand.

Uncle Redhead didn't waste a moment. He swiftly looped his end of the rope around Two-Eyes' shoulders. 'Pull, Two-Eyes! Pull!' he shouted.

Two-Eyes threw his weight against the rope, and in a moment Littlenose was sitting on the grass at the edge of the ravine, still holding on to the hunting bag.

When the world had stopped spinning, and he had got his breath back, Littlenose said, 'Which way do we go now?'

'We follow the river again,' said Uncle Redhead, 'until we get to a special place.' He reloaded Two-Eyes with their gear, and led the way along a well-trodden trail which wound along the edge of the ravine.

As they marched, the ravine became

steadily wider and shallower. Soon it was no more than a high river-bank, with the river now flowing wide and deep. Uncle Redhead called a halt where the bank curved away from the main river to form a wide sandy bay. 'Here we are,' said Uncle Redhead. 'Light a fire. We'll have lunch before we start work.'

Littlenose rummaged in his hunting bag and inside his furs. 'Have you got the flints?' he asked.

'No,' said his uncle, 'you had them last when you lit the fire for breakfast.'

'Then they're lost,' said Littlenose. 'They must have dropped out when I fell off the log.'

'Hm,' said Uncle Redhead. 'We'll have to try something else.' He strode off into the nearby woods, and came back

carrying two pieces of wood. One was a finger-thick stick and the other was flat and the size of his hand. With his flint knife, Uncle Redhead trimmed the end of the stick, and carved a small hollow in the other piece. 'Now, we'll see,' he said.
He crouched down and started twirling the end of the stick in the hollow, between the palms of his hands.

Littlenose watched curiously. Suddenly he shouted, 'It's working! I'm sure I saw smoke!' Uncle Redhead paused, wiped the sweat from his brow, and went on twirling. This time there was no doubt. A fine wisp of smoke trickled from the hollow in the flat piece of wood.

'Quick,' gasped Uncle Redhead, 'get some dry grass, bark, leaves . . . anything that will burn easily.' Littlenose quickly gathered what he could find. He heaped the dry stuff around the smoking stick. A few sparks appeared. Then a red glow. Littlenose blew gently, and tiny flames began to flicker. Uncle Redhead sat back, red and panting. Littlenose carried the burning leaves and grass carefully over to the fire, which was soon burning briskly.

As they ate their lunch, Uncle Redhead said, 'Here's what I want you to do. Cut strips of bark from those willows over there and plait them into bark rope.'

Uncle Redhead and Two-Eyes went off among the trees. There was a lot of loud shouting and squealing. Then Two-Eyes came out from among the trees, urged on by Uncle Redhead as he dragged a tree-trunk tied to the rawhide rope. He did this another five times until six long pine-trunks lay on the sand by the water's edge.

Now Uncle Redhead took Littlenose's bark rope and began to lash the trunks together, side by side. 'There it is!' he said when he had finished.

'There is what?' asked Littlenose.

'Our raft!' said Uncle Redhead. 'I told you we wouldn't be walking all the way. The river will carry us . . . and in comfort!'

Uncle Redhead trimmed two long saplings into poles. After much heaving and tugging, the raft floated clear of the beach. Littlenose held it steady with one of the long poles while Uncle Redhead loaded their gear and, to Littlenose's wonder, a large rock! Two-Eyes took some persuading to go aboard.

'It's all right!' said Littlenose.

That's what he said about the log bridge, thought Two-Eyes to himself, but he waded out and heaved himself on to the raft.

Uncle Redhead pushed against the sand with his pole. For a moment the raft scraped and bumped on the river-bed. Then it slid clear and moved gently out into the main current.

Littlenose watched the sandy bay dwindle in the distance. Ahead, the river flowed wide and strong, taking them farther on their journey to the south.

Voyage into Danger
Chapter 3

Travelling by raft was certainly easier than walking. It took a bit of care. There was not all *that* much room to move about, and if anyone moved at all, particularly Two-Eyes, the whole raft rocked violently. From time to time they steered in towards the shore and tied up while they gathered fruit and Two-Eyes grazed. Fish could be speared without leaving the raft. It was all very convenient. Littlenose asked Uncle Redhead what they would do if it rained.

'Get wet!' said Uncle Redhead with a shrug.

One evening it did rain. They were just about to go ashore for the night when black clouds rolled up, hiding the setting sun. Uncle Redhead guided the raft under the drooping canopy of an ancient willow-tree, and they slept snug and dry.

In the morning they climbed on to the river-bank. Littlenose prepared breakfast while Uncle Redhead searched about among the rocks by the water's edge. Presently he returned to the raft, staggering under the weight of an enormous flat stone. He laid it in the centre of the raft beside the rock they had brought from the sandy bay.

He straightened up, left the raft again, and began to gather armfuls of sticks and small logs. These he piled beside the flat stone.

Looks like he's gathering firewood, thought Littlenose.

'Firewood!' said Uncle Redhead as he sat down to breakfast. 'From here on it might not be too safe to go ashore.'

Even as he spoke there came a distant shout. Then another! Then a whole chorus! There was a crashing in the undergrowth, getting closer by the moment.

'It's not safe right this minute!' cried Uncle Redhead. 'Quick! On to the raft!'

A mob of ferociously painted figures appeared on the bank, screaming and yelling after the raft as the current quickly carried it out of reach.

'Straightnoses?' cried Littlenose.

'Just one of the more unpleasant tribes I told you about,' said Uncle Redhead. 'From now on we only go ashore for food and firewood. At night we'll anchor in the river and make a fire on the raft to cook by.'

The unpleasant tribesmen followed the raft for some distance along the river-bank, but were very quickly left behind, their ferocious cries fading in the distance.

And as Uncle Redhead had said, they spent the night out on the river, well clear of the bank. The large rock, fastened to the end of Uncle Redhead's rawhide rope, make an efficient anchor, while the flat

stone prevented the cooking fire from setting the logs of the raft on fire. They saw no more tribes, unpleasant or otherwise, but Two-Eyes trumpeted loudly at a herd of mammoths which had come down to the river to drink. And on another occasion a trip ashore for firewood came to an abrupt end when a fierce forest bull burst from the trees. It splashed through the water after the raft. As Littlenose pushed off, the bull caught his pole with its horns. The pole broke, and Littlenose almost fell into the water. Long after it was lost to sight round a bend in the river, the angry bull could be heard bellowing after them.

'Is it always like this, going south?' asked Littlenose. 'Bulls and unpleasant tribes, I mean. And blizzards and log bridges?'

'Yes,' said Uncle Redhead. 'Sometimes it's worse. We've had it very easy so far.'

'Oh!' said Littlenose.

Uncle Redhead had been watching the river-banks carefully for some time. 'We leave the river soon,' he said. 'Just checking landmarks. The bend after next leads to rapids and a high waterfall. As soon as we reach the *next* bend in the river we must make for the shore. Then we go on on foot.'

The raft was moving much faster than before as it came up to the bend. Uncle Redhead looked worried. Littlenose began to feel scared.

'Oh dear!' cried Uncle Redhead. 'I must have missed one of the landmarks! Quick! Make for the bank!'

Littlenose pushed hard with the remaining pole. Already the raft was rolling and pitching as the water grew rougher. Spray was breaking over them as they drew slowly nearer to the bank. The raft was still some distance out when Uncle Redhead shouted, 'We'll have to jump for it! Come on!'

He grabbed his hunting bag and leapt into the river. The water came to his waist and almost swept him off his feet.

Shouting 'Follow me, Two-Eyes!' Littlenose went next. He lost his footing, and came up spluttering. Uncle Redhead took his hand, and together they stumbled through the waves and on to the bank.

But where was Two-Eyes?

Too terrified to move, the small mammoth huddled on the leaping and spinning raft. Littlenose and Uncle Redhead raced along the bank, shouting 'Jump! Jump, Two-Eyes!' Already the roar of the waterfall could be heard up ahead.

But Uncle Redhead was running as fast as he could, pulling his rawhide rope from his hunting bag as he ran. He scrambled along a fallen tree sticking out into the current, making a running loop in the rope as he did so. A quick whirl round his head, and the rope was flying through the air, the loop dropping neatly over Two-Eyes' head. A couple of turns round a branch of the fallen tree and Two-Eyes was plucked from the raft, to be dragged to the bank by Littlenose and Uncle Redhead. As the small mammoth stood with water streaming from his fur, the raft broke in pieces and vanished among the foaming waves of the rapids.

After a rest to dry out, Littlenose, Two-Eyes and Uncle Redhead set off. It was good to be walking again. Sitting on a raft was all right, but there was nothing like a good walk to stretch the legs, Littlenose thought. Walking also made you warm. Littlenose wiped his brow. Out of the river breeze, it was really quite warm ... not to say hot.

He said so to Uncle Redhead:

'It's turned hot, hasn't it?'

'What did you expect?' said Uncle Redhead. 'That's why we've come south, isn't it? Time to change into our summer furs, I think.'

'It's a queer thought,' said Littlenose to himself. 'Here am I in my summer furs, and back home everyone will be wrapped up to the eyes against the cold.'

With every day that passed, the weather grew warmer. Even the country looked different. The trees seemed greener and the flowers brighter. Birds and butterflies in the air and beetles and lizards among the stones were coloured like nothing Littlenose had ever imagined.

They left the woods behind and crossed grassy plains. They climbed gently rolling hills and round the foot of high mountains. One night they made camp for the night high on a grassy hill. Littlenose was fast asleep when he was woken by Two-Eyes poking him with his trunk. 'Go to sleep, Two-Eyes,' said Littlenose. But Two-Eyes made a whimpering noise and nudged him again.

Uncle Redhead woke. 'Two-Eyes senses something,' whispered Littlenose. Uncle Redhead looked out into the night and listened. Crickets sang in the bushes, and an owl hooted. Then they heard it. A far-off rumbling. And at the same moment Littlenose said, 'The ground! I felt it move!' Two-Eyes squealed as everything shook and loose stones rolled down the hillside. After a moment, the rumbling and shaking stopped. Uncle Redhead led the way farther up the hill and pointed. Far away in the night was a red glow, from the centre of which flames and sparks suddenly shot into the sky.

'Old Grumbler!' said Uncle Redhead in a hushed voice. Nobody felt like going back to sleep but sat huddled together until daybreak, listening to the angry sounds from Old Grumbler and wondering what had happened to upset him.

They broke camp before it was properly light. As they came down out of the hills, there on the horizon was Old Grumbler's mountain. There were no sparks or flames, but a tall plume of dark smoke rose from the summit and drifted away on the morning breeze.

They were so busy watching the mountain that it wasn't until there was a loud shout that they realised that they were not alone. A crowd of people was straggling up the trail towards them. They were dusty and dishevelled. Many wore bandages, and several limped badly.

'I don't think this is one of the unpleasant tribes,' said Littlenose.

'*Unhappy*, I'd say,' said Uncle Redhead. 'I wonder what happened to them.'

He went up to the leader of the tribe. 'Been in a spot of bother?' he asked.

'Old Grumbler,' replied the man. 'Shook all our caves down in the night. We were lucky to get out in one piece . . . well, more or less in one piece! How about *your* caves?'

'Oh, we don't come from round here,' said Uncle Redhead. 'Just passing through.'

There was silence for a moment, then an old man with his arm in a sling and a bandage on his head said, 'That's it! Strangers! Old Grumbler doesn't like strangers! It's all *their* fault!'

The tribe began to mutter, and looked like being unpleasant after all as they crowded round in a very threatening manner. And to make it worse Old Grumbler let out a particularly angry-sounding rumble and shot a burst of flame out of the top of his mountain. And, for once, Uncle Redhead was at a loss for words!

It was Littlenose who, to his own

surprise, found himself saying, 'Well, if it's *our* fault, *we'd* better do something about it. Like telling Old Grumbler that we're sorry; that we didn't know he disliked strangers in his land.'

Uncle Redhead still didn't say anything.

Littlenose went on, 'I'll go now, by myself. You wait here, Two-Eyes. It might be dangerous.' He took his hunting bag from Two-Eyes' back and slung it on his shoulder. 'I'll be back as soon as I can,' he called back. Then he was out of sight, striding in the direction of the angrily-smoking mountain.

Beyond the Sea
Chapter 4

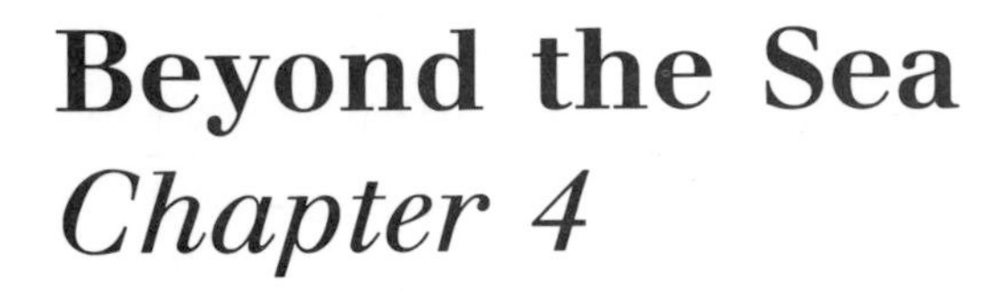

As Littlenose disappeared in the direction of Old Grumbler and his smoking mountain, the old man with the sling and the bandage said, 'Well, that's the last we're likely to see of him!'

'Sure enough,' said someone else. 'My uncle went to speak to Old Grumbler and we never saw him again. Young Strongarm came back, of course, but his hair was white as snow and he never spoke a sensible word to the end of his days!'

'We must stop Littlenose before it's too late,' cried Uncle Redhead at last. At which point the ground gave an extra-violent heave, knocking everyone off their feet.

'It's already too late,' said the leader of the tribe as they picked themselves up. 'Old Grumbler knows he's on his way. All we can do is wait.'

Meanwhile, Littlenose was striding towards the mountain. He reached the foot at nightfall. The country round about was scorched and blackened, and foul-smelling smoke filled the air and made his eyes water. He ate some food from his hunting bag before curling up to sleep among a pile of rocks, while high above a fiery glow lit the sky, and the ground trembled beneath him.

Before dawn, Littlenose was awake and toiling up the side of the mountain. It wasn't particularly steep, but underfoot was hot and cindery. Smoke poured from cracks in the rock. Pools of boiling mud seethed and bubbled. Close to the top Littlenose paused to rest, rubbing his eyes and coughing in the smoke. What was Old Grumbler like, he wondered? He imagined some sort of bad-tempered giant. Perhaps a kind of enormous version of Father on one of his bad days. He scrambled up the last part of the slope. And there was no giant. Not even a medium-sized one!

Littlenose looked over a rim of scorched stone into a vast pit. The bottom of the pit boiled and bubbled with liquid fire. The far side was almost hidden by smoke and steam which rose up above the rim and was blown away from Littlenose by the wind. But there was no Old Grumbler that he could see!

Feeling very bold, he stood up on the rim. 'Old Grumbler!' he shouted, his voice echoing off the blackened rocks. 'This is Littlenose! If me and Uncle Redhead . . . I mean, if Uncle Redhead and I have annoyed you by travelling through your country, we're very sorry. But, I think it's a bit much going knocking people's caves down!'

With a roar, a fiery fountain shot high into the air above the floor of the pit. Littlenose ducked. But he still felt very brave. He cupped his hands to his mouth and shouted again, 'We won't come this way again . . . I promise. So you won't be annoyed and start hurting people!'

And, even as he spoke, the fire died down, the noise faded almost to nothing, and even the smoke seemed to be thinning out. With a last look, in the hope of catching a glimpse of Old Grumbler, Littlenose turned and made his way back down the mountain.

He rejoined Uncle Redhead, Two-Eyes and the tribe late in the day. They looked at him in wonder. 'You did it!' they said in hushed voices. The ground had stopped trembling, and the plume of smoke from the mountain was no more than a grey wisp against the sky.

'What's he like, Old Grumbler?' they wanted to know.

'I just couldn't describe him,' said Littlenose truthfully.

They parted next day. The tribe went off on a search for new caves, and Littlenose, Two-Eyes and Uncle Redhead continued their interrupted journey south.

The sun seemed to get hotter with every day that passed . . . hotter by far than the hottest summer day that Littlenose could recall. But the travelling was most pleasant. They crossed rolling grassy plains ablaze with flowers. They watched herds of horses, which looked much bigger than those hunted by the Neanderthal Folk back home. They hunted deer and boar for food, and hid in a tree to avoid a sabre-toothed tiger which had an idea of hunting them. Two-Eyes hid in the bushes.

Then, one afternoon, Uncle Redhead stopped and sniffed the breeze. 'Smell that,' he said.

Littlenose sniffed. The air had a coolness to it, and something Littlenose thought vaguely that he remembered from long ago. 'It's the sea!' he cried.

'It's *two* seas,' said Uncle Redhead. He pointed ahead to where, faintly in the haze, Littlenose could make out the shape of a mountain peak.

'It's white,' he said. 'Is it covered with snow?'

'No,' said Uncle Redhead. 'The rock is white. There's a warm sea to one side of it, and a cold sea to the other . . .

and some very strange creatures live on the rock itself. No, I won't say any more. Just wait and see!'

Two days later they stood at the foot of the white mountain. On one side it sloped steeply upwards. On the other it dropped straight down to the blue sea.

'Where's the other sea?' asked Littlenose.

'All in good time,' said Uncle Redhead. 'Time to make camp.'

They made a fire close to the foot of the mountain, and after some supper lay down to sleep. Littlenose couldn't get to sleep. He had the unpleasant feeling that they weren't alone. Two-Eyes was also restless. Littlenose rose and stirred the fire. He thought for a moment that it shone on several pairs of eyes. But he could hear nothing, and at last managed to fall asleep.

Littlenose woke suddenly. Something was moving. Right beside him. It was his hunting bag! It slid along the ground . . . pulled by a small, grey hand tugging at the shoulder strap! Littlenose leapt up with a yell. The small creature pulling the hunting bag dropped it and ran chattering away among the rocks.

'Uncle Redhead! Uncle Redhead!' yelled Littlenose again. 'A little grey man tried to steal my hunting bag! There's another one! There are dozens of them!'

Uncle Redhead laughed. 'These are the creatures I told you about. They look a lot like people, but they're not. The tribes in these parts call them *apes.* They're harmless . . . but will steal anything they can get their paws on.'

They ate breakfast with whole families of apes watching from nearby rocks, and Littlenose was glad when they packed up and went on their way once again.

They went some way around the foot of the mountain. Then they swung left and headed due south. When they halted at noon, the sun was directly ahead and much higher in the sky than it ever was back home. Uncle Redhead led the way into a shady grove of trees. He went off by himself for a moment. When he came back he was carrying half a dozen large, round, golden-coloured fruits.

'You've never tasted anything like this,' he said, handing one to Littlenose.

Littlenose took a bite. 'You're right!' he spluttered, spitting it out again. 'It's horrible!'

Uncle Redhead laughed. 'You peel the skin off first,' he explained. He peeled one

of the fruits and gave it to Littlenose. And he was right. It was like nothing Littlenose had ever tasted in his life, unbelievably sweet, with juice that ran down his chin. Two-Eyes had one. He ate it, skin and all, and seemed to enjoy it.

'The people in these parts have a name for them,' said Uncle Redhead, 'but it escapes me for the moment. We should be meeting the locals soon.'

They turned their backs on the view of the distant sea. Far away Littlenose could make out the white mountain where the apes lived. He took a few more steps. And there was the other sea! It looked quite different! It was an icy green and the waves broke in crashing showers of spray against the rocks along the shore.

'We're nearly there,' said Uncle Redhead, that night.

'Nearly where?' asked Littlenose.

'Where we're going to spend the winter. With old friends of mine. I thought we might have met them by now, but I expect we'll see them tomorrow. And we've work to do.'

'Another raft?' asked Littlenose.

'A hut,' said Uncle Redhead.

'What's a hut?' asked Littlenose.

'Wait and see,' replied Uncle Redhead. 'Good night.'

They were eating breakfast next morning when Uncle Redhead suddenly jumped to his feet and shouted, waving his hand. A group of men was approaching. They weren't Neanderthal. But they weren't Straightnose either. Flatnose seemed a better description. They had dark skins and carried spears with bone spear-heads. Two of them had long pieces of wood with some sort of cord which bent the wood into a curved shape.

Uncle Redhead and the men shook hands, slapped each other on the back and talked excitedly with much laughter.

Littlenose caught his name and Two-Eyes', but could make out nothing else. He realised that these people spoke a foreign language. Uncle Redhead obviously spoke it too!

Uncle Redhead introduced Littlenose, who shook hands and said, 'Very pleased to meet you, sir,' to each of them in turn. They grinned at him, and he smiled back.

Two-Eyes was also introduced. And the men went wild with delight, stroking and patting him. Two-Eyes enjoyed the attention, particularly when they gave him one of the golden fruits. Littlenose caught a word that sounded like 'ornj'.

Now Littlenose, Two-Eyes and Uncle Redhead followed their new friends down from the ridge. They left them in a clearing among some thin woods.

'We camp here tonight,' said Uncle Redhead. 'And in the morning we present ourselves to the local chief. Tomorrow will be a very busy day. Get a good night's sleep.'

But Littlenose was already curled up, doing that very thing!

A New Tribe
Chapter 5

Littlenose woke to hear the sound of voices . . . children's voices! He sat up. Uncle Redhead was already up and about somewhere, but Littlenose was not alone. A crowd of children stood giggling and pointing. Suddenly, the children screamed and ran away. Properly awake now, Littlenose stood up. A dozen dark brown little faces watched from the bushes as Two-Eyes ambled up.

I think they're afraid of him, thought Littlenose. Haven't they ever seen a mammouth before? Then he remembered. They had probably never seen a mammouth with *fur!* He called Two-Eyes to him, and together they walked towards the bushes. The children backed away. But Littlenose called out, 'It's all right. This is Two-Eyes, my friend.' Two-Eyes trumpeted softly and waved his trunk. 'He wants to be your friend, too!'

The children didn't understand the words, but they crept forwards, and in a few moments were stroking Two-Eyes and speaking to him in their own language. Two-Eyes loved it. When Uncle Redhead appeared carrying fruit for breakfast Two-Eyes was trotting happily up and down with two of them riding on his back.

When they had eaten, Littlenose and Uncle Redhead tidied themselves in preparation for meeting the chief of the tribe. Then they walked a short distance to a wide clearing where the tribe was gathered. It was just like home . . . except for one thing. There were no caves!

'Where do people live?' whispered Littlenose.

'In huts,' said his uncle.

Littlenose looked round. All he could see was a circle of large piles of branches, leaves and grass. He wondered what they could be for. Before he had wondered very much, Uncle Redhead said, 'The chief.'

Back home, the chief of Littlenose's tribe was a kindly old gentleman with no teeth, very little hair, and on the portly side. *This* chief was a young man, tall and muscular. The tribe formed a circle about him, and he beckoned to Uncle Redhead and Littlenose. Then he made what sounded like a speech, and everyone smiled.

He next spoke to Uncle Redhead, who replied in his own language. The chief smiled and said a few words to Littlenose, who smiled back, wishing he knew what it was all about.

Then the crowd disappeared, and Uncle Redhead and Littlenose were left alone.

'What was all that about?' asked Littlenose.

'We have been welcomed to the tribe,' said Uncle Redhead, 'and allocated a place to build our hut. Come on.'

Littlenose followed his uncle. And he saw something he hadn't noticed before. People were coming and going through openings in the piles of grass and leaves. That was where they lived! These must be *huts!* How odd! The place for *their* hut was already marked out by a circle scratched in the ground. Uncle Redhead paced out five steps. 'Take Two-Eyes,' he said, 'and get tree branches *that* length and not more than two fingers thick.'

When he brought back the first load, Littlenose saw that Uncle Redhead had been hard at work with a sharp stick and a large stone making holes in the ground

round the edge of the circle. He took Littlenose's tree branches and began to stand them upright in the holes. A few more loads and the circle was complete. For a door there was a wider space at one side. With Littlenose's help, Uncle Redhead bent the branches down towards the centre and fastened them together with bark rope.

Thinner branches were interlaced with the others. Leafy branches and bundles of grass were tied to those. It was very tiring. Littlenose climbed on to Uncle Redhead's shoulders to fasten the highest pieces.

Then Uncle Redhead said, 'Well, that's that!'

Littlenose wiped the sweat from his eyes. The new hut looked magnificent. The noonday sun beat down on the clearing, but inside was cool and fragrant from the leaves and grasses. It was a great improvement on a rough, stony cave. But he couldn't help wondering how a hut would stand up to a bad-tempered black bear or a hungry sabre-toothed tiger! No doubt Uncle Redhead would have the answer to that one.

When they moved all their gear into the new hut, it was as if they had never lived anywhere else. For all practical purposes they were members of the tribe. Littlenose made friends with some boys of his own age, and even began to learn a few words of the language. Littlenose's best friend was Tiki, the son of the chief.

One evening Uncle Redhead said, 'I've a message for you from Tiki. He would like you to go hunting with him tomorrow. You might even learn something new.'

Littlenose doubted that very much. After

all, he *was* a junior hunter. He'd passed all his tests. However, he spent the time until bedtime getting a really sharp point on his flint-headed spear.

Tiki came soon after breakfast. He didn't have a spear, but he carried one of the curiously bent pieces of wood and cord. Slung over his shoulder he had a long leather pouch thing. Littlenose could have sworn that there were feathers sticking out from it. They left the huts behind and, on a patch of sandy ground, Tiki took a twig and drew an animal with horns and long legs.

'Ah,' said Littlenose, 'we're going to hunt deer.'

Tiki grinned and said something. The land was bare of cover except for occasional small trees and clumps of bushes. Tiki broke off a large leafy branch and by signs told Littlenose to do the same. Then he led the way forward, watching the ground as he went. He held up his hand and signalled for Littlenose to lie down. Together they crawled up a slight rise. There, well out of spear-shot, was a herd of small deer-like animals. Tiki stuck his leafy branch upright in the ground. So did Littlenose.

We're not close enough, thought Littlenose. Nobody could throw a spear that far. Perhaps he's waiting for them to move closer.

But Tiki wasn't waiting for anything. He had unslung the strange leather pouch and was taking out what looked like a miniature spear. It was only the length of Littlenose's arm . . . and had feathers at one end. The Neanderthal Folk sometimes put feathers on their spears, but only for decoration, not for hunting. Tiki was now kneeling behind his leafy branch. He held the curved stick by one hand in the middle. With the other hand he fitted the cord into a small notch in the end of the small spear, then pulled it back so far that the piece of wood bent even further. There was a loud *twang!* and a *whizz!* and Littlenose jumped. The spear had vanished. And so had the herd of deer.

Except one. Tiki ran over to the plump antelope which lay dead on the ground.

Tiki pulled out the little spear and said something. Littlenose caught something which sounded like 'aro', but he couldn't be sure. Littlenose wondered if perhaps it was magic. But he didn't really think so. He would have to learn more about this way of hunting.

He was helping Tiki to lift the deer on to his shoulders to carry it home when he heard a sound . . . a horribly familiar sound! Watching from an uncomfortably short distance was a woolly rhinoceros. Again it gave a loud snort made by woolly rhinoceroses when they were in a bad mood. Except that this rhinoceros wasn't woolly! It had dusty grey skin, all folds and wrinkles. It lowered its head and pawed the ground.

'Run!' cried Tiki, dropping the dead antelope.

But there was nowhere to run to. The trees were few, and not much more than large bushes.

Then the rhino charged!

'Don't move!' shouted Littlenose.

He didn't have a hunting robe, but he grabbed the two leafy branches and ran towards the angry beast, shouting at the top of his voice. 'Get out! Go away! Go and frighten someone your own size!'

Uncle Redhead had said that woolly rhinoceroses were cowards and bullies. Littlenose hoped that *unwoolly* ones were the same. *This* one was short-sighted as well as deaf! It didn't notice Littlenose until it was almost upon him. It gave a sudden startled squawk and swerved to one side. It tripped over its own feet and almost fell. Still shouting at the top of his voice, Littlenose struck out with one of the branches. It caught the rhinoceros on the side of the nose. This was too much. It blundered round until it was facing the way it had come, then galloped off in a thick cloud of dust until it was lost to view.

Littlenose returned to the huts to a hero's welcome. Tiki was shouting to everyone about his exploit, and the people came running. They shook him by the hand.

They clapped him on the back. The chief came out and made a speech, while Uncle Redhead stood and smiled proudly at his nephew.

Uncle Redhead translated the chief's speech. 'He has adopted you,' he told Littlenose. 'As long as you are living with the tribe, you will be treated as if you were his son.'

Littlenose left the huts and wandered off to sit with his back against a tree. It was very like the favourite tree he had at home where he did all his special thinking. Two-Eyes appeared and lay at his feet.

'Since I left home with Uncle Redhead to come south for the winter so much has happened that I'm not sure that some of it isn't a dream. I've travelled by raft. I've spoken to a giant in a fiery mountain. I've seen little grey men called apes ... who aren't men at all. I've built a hut. At least, I've helped build a hut. And I've seen a woolly rhinoceros without any wool. I haven't met any black men yet, but I'm sure I will. And now I have an extra father, who's a chief. And, if he's adopted me, then that means he's adopted you too, because we always do things together.'

Two-Eyes hadn't thought of that. He felt rather pleased.

'I'm going to enjoy myself here,' Littlenose went on. 'And, of course, I'll enjoy returning home in the spring. But that's a long way off.'

He looked at the sky. The sun was sinking, and here in the south darkness came down very quickly. 'It's been a busy day, Two-Eyes,' he said. 'I think it's time for bed.'

And he went back to the hut to sleep, and to dream of all the wonderful things he would do in the weeks to come.